Tainted Beginnings

A Dark Syndicate Novella

Khardine Gray

Faith Summers

The following story contains mature themes, strong language and sexual situations.

It is intended for mature readers. All characters are 18+ years of age and all sexual

acts are consensual.

Tainted Beginnings

Khardine Gray
writing as
USA Today Bestselling Author
Faith Summers

Dark Romance Note

Author Note

Please note Faith Summers is the Dark romance pen name of USA Today Bestselling Author Khardine Gray

Reader note:

Tainted Beginnings is a novella that falls part of my Dark Syndicate world.

One wild night in Vegas led me here...

I should have known Nick was the devil when he first smiled at me.

But I couldn't resist the irresistible.

Especially when the devil came in the form of a sinfully hot Italian man that looked like he stepped out of a forbidden fantasy.

Of course, I said yes, when he asked me to spend the night with him.

After all, this was Vegas.

I came here to forget the disaster at home with my ex-husband and former best friend.

The night I spent with Nick was perfect.

Until I saw him do something I shouldn't have seen.

I ran to protect myself.

But what happened in Vegas followed me home.

Now I'm in danger.
And he's the only one who can save me...

Chapter One

Nick

I scan the crowd once more and sigh with frustration.

He's not here.

I know Federico. He's never late to anything. It's not his style. So, if we've been here for over three hours and haven't seen him or one of his fucktards yet, it means he's not coming.

Like most of the men in my circle, the Marchesi is one of the places he visits when he's in Vegas.

I always stay here when I'm in town. The hotel has become sort of a neutral ground for the underworld, because like the other famous hotels on the Strip, it attracts some of the world's elite.

I'm sure between Leo and me, we have looked everywhere we could. The ground-floor casino was the last area to check, and I've scanned it three times to be certain I checked the place out properly.

We've also been here long enough to pick up on anything amiss, even though Vegas is constantly busy.

Since nothing gets past me, I can say with certainty that nothing is going to happen tonight, which means we'll have to go back to the drawing board.

This is the kind of shit that happens when you have to rely on information from underground snitches like Benji who can't get their facts straight. If he weren't as loyal to the D'Agostinos as my family and I have been, I'd be inclined to think the fucker was screwing with us. But what he gave us is what he had.

To his knowledge, Federico DiMaggio was supposed to be in Vegas tonight at the Grand Marchesi. Either Leo or I was supposed to make the hit on this kill on sight job.

This mark is one I've been itching to hit since Federico killed Antonio. Antonio was one of the best enforcers in our crew. More than anything, he was like a brother to me and helped me avenge the deaths of my family.

This mission is personal for me. Not just a job. It's pissing me right the fuck off that Antonio has been dead for six weeks now, and we're still looking for Federico.

I make my way over to the furthest wall by the upper-deck bar, so I can have some privacy to talk to Leo. Taking out my phone, I find his number and call him.

He answers on the first ring.

"I got nothing up here, Leo," I say. "Not a damn thing."

"Same here. What should I do now, *boss*?" He chuckles, placing emphasis on the word 'boss.'

Following Antonio's death, Massimo D'Agostino, the head boss of the L.A. Syndicate and leader of the D'Agostino family, upgraded me to senior enforcer. The guys tease me about it at every chance because I'm the most reckless of the group. I get my shit done, though. That's all that matters. I was also trained by my father, who was the best.

Prior to Antonio, it was Father who held that position. The men in my family have worked with the D'Agostinos for many generations. I'm the last one left, so I take pride in the position.

"Go over the footage and reports on where Federico was last seen," I answer. "Something's off, and we need to figure out what it is before this gets back to L.A. I think either he knows we're here, or he has other plans."

"Leave it with me."

"Good. I'll let Massimo know what's happening. I don't think we're going to find anything in Vegas."

"Alright, I'll report back later."

We hang up, and my gaze instantly drifts across to the group of ladies sitting around a table on the floor below me.

I zero in on the beautiful redhead who reminds me of a cross between an erotic mermaid and a shy librarian.

She looks shy; I'd bet she's not, though.

A woman as sexy as her shouldn't be. It would be a crime if she were, and a real shame for a guy like me.

As tonight was a bust, and I don't have any other plans, I see no harm in making use of my time here in Vegas in other ways.

I head to the balcony to get a better look at the beauty and rest my hands on the glossy black rails.

I first saw her when she walked in with her friends. There are four of them sitting at the table. Two brunettes, a blonde, then her. The sexy mermaid stood out amongst the group and this sea of people.

I'm not sure what it was exactly about her that caught my attention. Yes, she's beautiful. Hollywood gorgeous. And that mid-length, figure-hugging navy dress she's wearing with those fuck-me heels screams exactly that—fuck me.

There are many beautiful women here, and I've fucked even more, but what got my attention was the spark I saw in her eyes when she looked at me. It was brief, but it was there.

She looked away first and was right to. That would have been her innate instincts telling her to stay away from me. All beings have those instincts when faced with danger. Listening to the warning keeps them safe and away from dark creatures like me.

I'm a very bad man, and she looks like a good girl.

She looks like the kind of woman I should never touch. And that just makes me want her even more.

As she lifts her pretty, little head and her gaze collides with mine, I see that spark again.

This time, she doesn't look away as quickly, and I feel more like the devil I am for holding her gaze and making a point of ensuring she knows it's her I'm looking at.

We're about thirty feet apart, but the magnetism of the attraction rippling between us makes it feel like she could be standing right next to me.

I might not have found the man I came to kill, but I found her.

And I'm going to end tonight with her in my bed and those long legs wrapped around me as I pound into her.

Chapter Two

Tennessee

As heat creeps into my cheeks and races down the length of my body, I look away from the ridiculously handsome stranger staring back at me.

I only looked back because I could feel eyes on me like I did before when I first saw him. I wanted to know if the heated gaze I could feel boring into me belonged to him—it did. I also *only* kept looking because I wanted to see if he was truly watching me and not someone else. Like one of my friends, my cousin, or the ladies behind me.

After you've gone through the type of shit I have, you start to doubt yourself.

And *everything*.

And...every man.

Now that I've confirmed he's definitely looking at me, I wish I hadn't indulged in the temptation to stare because now I know he's even more gorgeous than I thought.

And now that I've basically eye-fucked him, I've embarrassed myself.

It's just that I wouldn't have believed a guy like him could be looking at me. There's no way I'm his type. He looks like the kind of man who would have a

supermodel or some Hollywood starlet on his arm.

Like all the other men here, he looks suave in what can only be an Armani suit. But the way he wears it, so casually and effortlessly, as if he's in a Davidoff advert, takes the definition of sexy to another hemisphere.

His short, cropped hair draws all the attention to the chiseled features of his face, he's got powerful shoulders built for the military and a body with the type of muscles that have evidently been through hours of training.

Although he has light hair, I guessed from his olive skin and Mediterranean features he must be Italian, and my God, does he confirm what my aunt Grace-Anne says about European men—that they have this classy passion about them that could melt your panties with one look.

I'm sure mine are barely hanging on to my hips.

God... I am far too worked up, and I need to calm down.

"I saw that," Bree bubbles, pouring on her Southern accent that's just a fraction tamer than mine and Georgia's.

"Saw what?" It's best I pretend I don't know what she means.

"You know what," Quinn cuts in, shaking her head at me while Georgia nods with mischief glittering her eyes.

"We all saw him looking at you, sugar, so don't deny it." Georgia giggles

"People are allowed to look at each other." I try to sound

nonchalant, but I barely pass. "That's what eyes are for, right?"

"Also for assessing your next hookup. And believe me when I say he was totally checking you out."

Their heads all bobble in unison like dashboard dollies.

"Girls, please."

"Don't you dare 'girls, please' us." Bree lifts her chin and rivets her gaze to mine. "Remember the conditions of this trip."

"How could I forget."

Open mind.

That was the promise I made before we boarded the plane. I was to keep an open mind to all possibilities and adventures that came from being here, and I wasn't to shy away from anything like I have been all year.

Honestly, my head is still all over the place after this week's debacle, so I probably would have agreed to anything.

Vegas is the last place I should be. I'm not here to hook up. Okay—yes, according to my friends, I am, but I'm not.

I can't.

My presence in Sin City is only to humor them and show my appreciation for their support. Each of them has been my rock during this difficult, horrible time of my life, and I would have felt guilty if I hadn't said yes to this girls' getaway. They each have busy lives yet organized this weekend just to cheer me up.

Quinn and Bree both have husbands and babies back in Wilmington—the place I used to call home.

Georgia is my cousin but is more like a sister to me. So, while she'll claim it was a given she would always support me, she didn't have to.

Above everything, I'll admit the thing that pushed me to come here the most was their loyalty to me.

When I found out Kurt, my now ex-husband, was cheating on me with Mary, my now ex-best friend, there was a clear divide in our group of friends.

The girls and their counterparts chose me.

No one will ever know what that meant to me.

I've known Quinn, Bree, and Mary since we were kids. Quinn and Bree have always been close. Mary was that for me. Mary and I were so close our husbands worked together at the law firm.

She worked for them both as their secretary, and that's probably how the affair began. Although my heart tells me it began before they started working together, and I was just the blind fool.

"Remember, the purpose of this trip is to let go of the shit that happened in Wilmington," Quinn points out, cutting into my thoughts. "Besides, it's been nice hanging out. Now that you're going to be in Charlotte, we won't see you as much."

A pang of guilt pulls at my insides when I think of my move. Charlotte isn't that far from Wilmington but far enough with a three-hour drive on a good day without traffic. For the last couple of years, we've been as close as we all were in high school. The last two days spent here in Vegas proved that we were the same bunch of crazy girls—even without Mary.

I'll be working with Georgia in her catering company as a joint owner. We've already signed contracts. The only thing to come out of my acrimonious divorce is the money.

Kurt comes from an uber-wealthy family anyway, but

he's also one of the top lawyers in this country. I put the money from my share of the divorce settlement into this new venture with Georgia and starting over—whatever that might mean for me.

The first step was moving. There was no way I could stay in Wilmington after what happened. It's not as small as some of the other towns in North Carolina, but the gossip is just as toxic.

"It would be great to see you have some fun while we're here together," Quinn adds, giving me a saucy smile.

"Depends on what kind of fun you mean." I know what kind of fun she's talking about. I just can't remember what fun like that feels like.

I'm going to jump ahead and guess that any fun with a man like Mr. Perfect would be the sort to land me in sinful trouble.

"Tennessee Patterson, we're all big girls here," Bree declares. "You know what sort of fun we mean. This isn't even the case of forgetting one guy with another. It's a necessity."

I laugh. Trust Bree to come up with something like that.

"How is it a necessity?" I incline my head to the side.

"Because we can't allow you to slip into the shadows. This trip is about living it up." Bree nods enthusiastically. "So, if a gorgeous guy is looking at you, work with it."

Georgia suddenly tugs on my arm. "You better work with it real fast because he's heading this way."

"What?" My nerves scatter like mice when the light pops on in a dark room.

My heart jumps into my throat when I see the drop-dead gorgeous Italian god definitely heading this way, and his eyes are practically glued to me in a way that could strip me bare layer by layer.

My heart is still in my throat when he stops by Quinn and Bree and smiles.

That smile should have come with some warning because it's sinful and full of lust.

"Evening, ladies," he begins. His voice holds a slight accent that adds to his allure.

"Hi," they all say.

I can't talk; my lips part, though, as if I'm going to. The words just don't come.

"Sorry to intrude on your get-together. I wondered if I might borrow your friend if she doesn't mind being borrowed." He keeps his gaze on me, and I don't know what the hell to think.

"She doesn't mind," Georgia says before anyone else can answer, and he switches his gaze to her. "But this is my cousin. So, before she goes anywhere with you, I'd like to see some ID first."

I'm surprised at Georgia. I thought she'd be the first to hand me away like the prized turkey at Thanksgiving.

"My name is Nick Bellotto," he answers with a smirk. I was right. He's Italian. He pulls out his driver's license and walks over to Georgia and me. He gives

her the license, and she carefully inspects it.

"You're from L.A.?"

"I am. How about you keep this." Now he pulls out a business card.

She takes that, too. "You're a consultant?" Georgia looks impressed.

"Yes. And the owner of the casino will vouch for me as a good guy. Did I pass?" He raises a brow.

"You did."

When the three of them nod, he gives me his undivided attention, and I find myself lost in his dark brown eyes.

"What's your name, goddess?"

Goddess. Wow. I've never been called that before.

"It's Tennessee Patterson." I try not to stutter. My brain still stumbles over using my maiden name, even though I returned to it months ago.

No one would believe by looking at this shell of a person I've become that I was once the 'it girl' and the life of our group. It used to be me encouraging the others to get a life, have open minds, and seize the moment.

"Pleasure to meet you, Tennessee. So, do you want to come and join me for a drink?"

Out the corner of my eye I can tell his forwardness has definitely scored points with Georgia, who is nodding her head off. She definitely wholeheartedly approves.

What about me, though?

Can I just go with him?

I can. But should I?

He's not looking at me like he just wants to have a drink. And... when I stare back at him, I can't lie and say I'm thinking about drinking at all.

But there's a dangerous vibe about him that the old me senses. It warns me to stay away. Except the sex appeal he oozes numbs my brain and entices me to forget my life and escape with him.

Nick leans slightly closer, and I inhale his rich masculine scent.

He smells like passion and power. Like the formidable pine trees in the forest back home. Like sandalwood and sex.

"Come on, I promise I won't bite, unless you want me to." He winks at me, and the butterflies in my stomach go crazy.

It's one drink. One break. One moment of reprieve for my tired soul that truly needs the reminder of fun.

Who could resist a sinfully gorgeous man who looks like he stepped out of a dark fantasy?

So, when Nick puts out his hand, I take it.

Chapter Three

Tennessee

With his hand placed at the small of my back, Nick leads me to the VIP lounge of the club in the hotel.

The décor is breathtaking with stunning black leather sofas and glossy slate varnished floors with a marble effect.

It's just us in here along with the bartender. When he notices us walk in, he approaches with a decanter and a bottle of expensive-looking wine with an Italian name I won't even try to pronounce.

Nick starts speaking Italian to him, and I watch, trying to decipher what they're talking about. Eventually, the bartender nods, sets the decanter down on the little table between the sofas, and returns the bottle of wine to the bar.

"What did you say to him?" I ask Nick when he looks at me.

"He brought us a bottle of Brunello di Montalcino."

God, his accent. I swear I've never heard anything sexier in my life. "Oh, right, and that was a bad thing because?"

"Have you ever had that wine before?"

"No, I most definitely have not." I chuckle lightly, and his gaze drops momentarily to my lips.

"Brunello di Montalcino is a strong red wine. It's earthy and takes some getting used to. I figured you for something a little sweeter." He looks me up and down, taking no caution to hide the fact that he's checking me out.

Kurt was never like that, and since I've never been with anybody else, I'm not exactly knowledgeable on different types of men.

"What made you think that?"

He turns his smile up a notch. "Because you look like you taste sweet."

All I can do is stare back at him and pray my pale skin isn't giving me away and turning as red as my hair.

"Do you say that to all the women you meet in Vegas?" I try to summon that nonchalance I had going on downstairs when I was with the girls.

"No."

I'm sure that's not true, but it doesn't matter. Right now, this man has me hooked, and I don't care about anything else.

"After you." He motions for me to sit on the larger sofa.

I do, and he sits next to me. The bartender comes back with another bottle of wine, to which Nick nods.

When the bartender pours us each a drink in the long-stemmed wine glasses, Nick picks one up and holds it up to my lips.

"Taste this," he says. The smile he gives me now emphasizes the dimple in his left cheek, and I struggle not to swoon over his good looks like a teenage girl with a crush on the most popular boy at school.

I dip my head and breathe in the floral scent before taking a sip of the fruity cherry- and raspberry-flavored wine. The moment the liquid hits my tongue, all my tastebuds awaken and come alive. It's delicious and quite unlike anything I've ever had before.

"Wow, what is that?" I'm genuinely intrigued.

"Brachetto. Was I right about the sweetness?"

"You were."

His eyes take me in again, and he looks like he wants to taste me. The thought of a stranger doing something like that to me should make me run the other way, but it doesn't.

It makes moisture bead between my thighs, and this is not the type of dress to get aroused in.

"Have more." He hands me the glass, and I drink a little more, savoring the flavor. "It's from the Piedmont region in Italy. My family is from there."

"Really? That sounds exciting. I've never been to Italy."

"You'd like it." He looks at me like he knows I would. I don't doubt him because Italy is one of the places I've always wanted to visit.

"I'm sure I would. I suppose now I don't have to ask you about your accent."

"I guess not. What about yours?"

I smile. "Do you want to guess?"

He narrows his eyes, takes a sip of his drink, and sets the glass back on the table. "Tennessee from Tennessee, but you don't live there anymore."

"Spot on. How'd you guess? People say my accent isn't as strong as it used to be."

"I have off-the-chart attention-to-details skills, and I'm good with accents."

"That's impressive." I'm only saying that because it is impressive. If he weren't as sexy as he is, I'd be inclined to think he was trying to impress me, but men like him don't have to try.

"Grazie."

"I moved to North Carolina when I was little."

"I've never been there. Sounds like a nice place, though."

"It is."

"So, what brings you to Vegas, Tennessee?"

On to business—or maybe it's more like pleasure. And suddenly, I feel more awkward than I already did. I knew this question would come up, though. It was a given.

"Maybe the same reason as everyone else. *Fun.*" I might have believed myself more if I'd said that with a little more oomph. "Aren't you here for fun?"

He tilts his head to the side. "Not until I saw you."

I *am* blushing now. I can feel it sweeping over me from head to toe.

"Is that so?"

"It is."

"So, what were you here for before you saw me?" I can't believe I said that without revealing how nervous I am.

"Work."

"Consulting?"

He nods. "Let's just say I'm a special kind of consultant. Back to you."

"I assure you I'm not that interesting."

"There's no way I'm going to believe that."

"You're too kind."

"You wouldn't think so if you knew me." That dangerous vibe returns, flickering within his eyes with a dark menace that ignites my wariness. However, it's quickly extinguished by my curiosity to know what this man might find so interesting about me. "Don't tell me there's a Mr. Tennessee. If there is, I might have to fight him for you."

When laughter falls from my lips, I'm shocked at myself. I've laughed with the girls, but that was me simply trying to put my best face forward. Just now was a glimmer of my old self.

The woman I haven't been, if I'm honest, for years.

"There's no Mr. Tennessee anymore," I tell him.

"What happened to him?"

"He cheated on me with my best friend and got her pregnant." That was probably too much to tell, but it sums up perfectly everything that happened and is still happening.

The glint in his eyes dulls, and there's a tick in his jaw like he could be incensed to hear what happened to me. It's a nice thought to imagine a guy like him feeling anything toward me. Like he would truly fight for me and fight my battles.

I had never believed that Kurt would be my enemy. But he became that the moment I caught him with Mary. I unloved him in those seconds that passed, and what I felt since was rage. Not toward him but myself.

On our wedding day, I had what I thought was cold feet. But it wasn't that at all. The voice telling me I was going down the wrong path because I wasn't in love with him was trying to warn me away. At the time, I was eighteen and pregnant and scared. We got married for the wrong reasons, and that's why I felt rage.

I'm pulled from my sordid walk down memory lane when Nick inches closer and stops a breath away from my lips.

"Are they still together?"

"In some sort of way."

I don't know, and I don't care. Kurt is a fucking asshole who's made my life a living hell since the breakup because he wants me back, and there's not a chance in hell I'll be doing that.

Mary became the vindictive bitch who had the audacity to tell me the reason why Kurt went to her was because I couldn't have children.

It's amazing how people you trust turn ugly within minutes.

"Were you married to him?"

"Yes."

"How long?" He searches my eyes as if he's trying to find something.

"Fourteen years. Too long, right?"

"You don't look old enough to have been married for fourteen years." He smirks and presses a finger to the edge of my jaw.

"How old do you think I am?" I feel like I'm at least a hundred.

"Twenty-five."

I laugh again. "Sorry to disappoint you. I'm not some hot twenty-something-year-old. I'm thirty-one."

"Then you're a hot, extremely sexy thirty-one-year-old."

"Am I?"

"Yes, and he didn't deserve you."

"How do you know that?" I release the breath burning my lungs. "I could have been the evil bitch." I truly wish I had been.

Taking a lock of my hair, he lifts the ends and allows it to float back down to my arms.

"I just know, and you're not the evil bitch type. I'm not attracted to women like that."

"What are you attracted to, Nick Bellotto?"

"You. I know a good thing when I see it. I'm no more deserving of you than your asshole ex, except unlike him, I'm selfish enough to take you for myself."

Oh my God.

My brain numbs as if someone just placed it on a block of ice. There's no mistake now in his intention judging by his words and the way he's looking at me.

"Are...you?" Up until now, I thought I had a smooth flow going on—considering my nerves. Now that my brain has turned to glop and checked out on me, I'm floundering, and all I can feel is arousal.

"Yes. Does that scare you, Tennessee?"

Yes, it does. But I've been raised to never admit when you're scared. "Should it?"

"No, I can tell you're nervous. What makes you nervous about me?"

I think for a moment and try to even out my shallow breaths. "I don't know what you're thinking."

"Let me make it easier for you and show you."

Before I can think, he lowers his head and covers my lips with his. As our lips touch, it feels like someone threw fire on my skin, and he consumes me.

The sudden ignition parts my lips, and he sweeps his tongue into my mouth. I taste him, and suddenly I'm lost. I'm lost in madness. I'm lost in the escape I craved when I first saw him.

I'm lost in him.

He kisses me as if he's trying to take everything from me. Like he's hungry for me.

Shamelessly, I kiss him back with the same drive as if I've spent my life kissing him, and for the first time since my life turned inside out, I forget what happened to me.

Nick pulls out of the kiss, and I'm not ready for him to stop.

I shouldn't feel like that. We just met.

Before embarrassment takes over and I look like the starved, desperate divorcee I am, he cups my face, and all I focus on is his fingers on my skin.

"Just so we're clear and there's no room for confusion, I'm going to fuck you."

Fuck me?

My heart rate rises like a pressure cooker about to explode, and the tingle that was in my chest blasts all over my body.

The image of him fucking me fills my mind, and I can't shake it from my head.

"That okay with you?" He adds with a wink.

"Yes."

Chapter Four

Tennessee

We make it inside the private elevator, his lips devouring mine and my legs wrapped around his waist.

As we go up to God knows where, Nick pushes me into the wall and punishes my mouth with angry kisses like he hates me and wants me all at the same time.

He squeezes my breasts and runs his hands down to my ass, where he grabs a handful of my flesh.

My heart throbs in my throat when his fingers graze over the soft cotton fabric of my panties covering my pussy. It's then I realize my dress must have ridden so far up my hips that I'm exposed.

This isn't like me. I don't do these types of things. I've never done this. Kurt is the only man I've ever been with and —damn it, it's fucking time to stop thinking about him.

How could I be thinking about that asshole when I'm with this guy?

This man, who looks like God took his own sweet time to make him and added an extra helping of sexiness.

Nick's lips track down to my neck, and he shoves me up against the wall.

"Fuck it, I need you now," he growls against my ear.

My eyes widen when I realize what he means.

"Now?" I manage, barely able to speak through the pleasure taking over my being.

"Fuck, yeah."

"In here?"

"Yes, goddess."

He presses the red emergency button on the car, and we come to a stop.

Setting me down, he keeps one firm hand on my waist and the other on the wall beside my head.

"What if someone sees us on the cameras or something?"

"Those cameras were switched off the moment I stepped in."

What kind of man has that type of power? Clearly someone who doesn't exist in the same sphere as me.

He smooths his hands over the flat of my belly and traces a line with his thumb to the zipper on the side of my dress.

He pulls it down, and my dress peels away from me like a flower opening on the first morning of spring.

The heat glowing in his eyes holds me in place, and I'm almost afraid to breathe in case the fantasy fades and I wake up in the depression of my world.

He's real, though. He's not fading, and I'm not going anywhere either.

With one quick snap, he undoes my strapless bra, and my breasts spill out free of the restriction.

He looks at my nakedness and smiles, satisfied by what he sees. At that moment, I feel like a woman again. Like a desired woman.

Grabbing my hand, he presses it to the growing bulge of his cock pushing against his zipper.

"This is what you do to me and every other man I saw looking at you tonight," he says in a husky voice.

"Other men were looking at me?"

"Yes, but I'm the lucky guy who got you." He returns to my lips and fills his palms with my breasts; then he works his way down to take my right breast into his mouth.

He sucks hard on my nipple until it turns painfully hard; then he moves to my other breast and gives it the same attention. His wild suckle has me moaning in his arms, my mind shaken by the pleasure he gives me.

I barely manage to contain myself when he crouches down and cups my sex, then rolls my panties down my legs.

He pushes his face between my thighs and thrusts his tongue into my pussy to eat me out. Instantly, my body succumbs to the spiral of ecstasy that commands I give in to the raw pleasure assailing me.

I was still aware that people could possibly hear us, but the force of carnal need rushing through me robs me of caring, and mindless moans fall from my lips.

I need this. Fuck, I need him.

Grabbing on to his shoulders, I steady myself and allow him to consume me like I've never been consumed before.

"You taste like the finest meal, goddess," he says while

licking my clit. Then he starts talking in Italian, and my head spins.

I can't even think to ask him what he's saying in English. Then I decide I don't want to know. Whatever he's saying sounds like sweet nothings I could indulge in forever.

Suddenly, the stab of his fingers in my passage doubles me over, and all I can do is tighten my grip on his shoulders as a greedy, ravenous orgasm sweeps over me.

I cry out from the impact, and he smiles up at me, taking advantage of my position to lick the tips of my breasts as they bounce in his face.

When he stands, and I see the bulge of his cock has grown even bigger, I know it's time for him to fuck me.

He pushes his jacket down his shoulders, takes out a condom from his back pocket, then shoves his pants down his legs, unleashing his cock.

My mouth waters when I see the pre-cum beading at the tip of his bulbous head.

When he notices me looking, he catches my face, his rough grip kicking my heartbeat up a notch.

"I'm not a gentle man, Tennessee. I'm going to fuck you hard."

I gasp when his fingers lace through my hair, and he brings my lips back to his for a cruel, hard kiss.

When he's finished, he turns me to face the wall, and I hear the condom wrapper being torn open.

Moments later, he grips my hips, lines up the head of his cock with my entrance, and slams into my pussy so hard I see stars.

I had no reason to disbelieve him when he said he

wouldn't be gentle. I just never expected it to feel so wild and reckless.

Or to like it.

He pounds into me like a vicious beast, like earlier when he claimed my lips, like we're enemies and he hates me. He fucks me ruthlessly into the wall, and all I can do to stop myself from falling off the face of reality is press my hands against the smooth walls and let the moans fall from my lips.

I can't believe this is us, or that this is me.

Me, the former dutiful housewife who would never miss the Sunday service at church and this hot, wild man I don't know in this elevator. We never even made it to his room.

"You feel so fucking good, goddess," he grates out, pushing deeper into my body.

"Oh, God!" I scream as I come again.

He's the one who feels good. He feels good inside me, and outside of me.

The rush of electricity scorching my body slams into my soul, and I know after this, my world will never be the same again.

Suddenly, his merciless pounds turn into cold hardcore fucking, and time freezes, holding us there in the claws of passion I never want to leave.

Nick keeps me there, hammering into me until a ferocious growl rips from his throat and he climaxes, pressing his granite chest into my back as he fucks me into the wall one last time.

By the time he's finished, my head is so light, I actually might faint and fade away. That was crazy wild. I've never experienced anything so raw and insane.

Nick pulls out of me and turns me slowly to face him. As our gazes tangle, I wonder if this might be it.

The end of the night, the end of our meeting, the end of us.

I'd get my clothes back on and walk out of here, never to see him again.

That's what should happen, right? I don't know him, and he doesn't know me. I have a life to rebuild, or rather a fresh start to make. I've only just started taking those baby steps.

He lowers to kiss me, and the rational thoughts of reasoning fade from my mind as if they were never there.

"Ready for more?" he asks against my lips.

"More?" My breath catches. "You... still want me?"

"Oh yes, sweet Tennessee." He licks over my lips, and I bite back a smile, causing him to smile, too. "I've only just begun to taste you, and I'm starving for more. So much more. I want you all night. Can I have you?"

"Yes."

Chapter Five

Nick

As the beautiful mermaid woman takes my cock into her mouth, I lace my fingers through the silky-smooth fibers of her gorgeous red hair.

Jesus Christ, the jolt of raw pleasure lancing through me already has my balls tightening.

I already know this woman is not one I'm going to forget easily when this night is over.

I've already had her twice, and this is the prelude to round three.

Fuck, that mouth of hers is raw magic to my soul, and looking at her naked on her knees before me, sucking my cock, is what fantasies are made of.

I'm trying not to think too much past the insane buzz she's giving me that's more potent than any drug I've ever taken.

I'm the kind of monster who acts on impulse. I take what

I want, like the way I took her, and if someone pisses me off, I deal with them.

When she told me the brief details of what happened to her, it got to me, and I wanted to put her motherfucking ex in his place.

I shouldn't feel such indignation, but my crazy mind seems to have decided that she was mine the moment our lips touched.

I'm acting crazy, and since I've already had her, I should leave.

I just can't bring myself to do it.

She starts licking over my balls, confirming any thoughts of leaving need to go to the back of beyond; then her tongue glides over my shaft in rasping strokes, and I lose control.

I grab a handful of her silky hair and force her to take my dick deeper into her mouth. Like the good girl she is, she obeys and takes me as deep as she can until tears stream out the corners of those emerald eyes.

She's so fucking beautiful and even more so with her mouth full of my cock. She sucks like a slut, but this woman is so far from that.

My balls tighten, signaling make or break time. Either I allow her to suck me off and fill her mouth with cum, or I finish inside her.

If I wanted to forget her, I'd end this night in her mouth. But I want to own that tight little pussy again.

I want to feel her walls wrap around my dick like a glove while I tunnel into her.

Grabbing her arm, I pull her to stand, and she looks at me all doe-eyed with her lips swollen from my cruel punishment of her mouth.

Her tits bounce with the nipples puckered from her arousal, so I catch them between my thumbs and forefingers before I kiss her.

"Get on the bed. All fours, ass up," I order, nibbling on her bottom lip.

She responds by moving back to my lips for a quick kiss that feels completely outside the filthy things I've done to her and still plan to do to her.

The kiss is too innocent and chaste for me, but something inside me craves more moments like it after she turns away and makes her way over to the bed.

It's a reminder she doesn't belong in my world.

The moment she crawls onto the bed and I see that ass, my selfishness returns, and I decide all over again I'm going to keep her in my darkness.

With my aching cock straining to burst, I make my way over to her and roll on a condom. I have two left in the pack I plan to use with her.

I press my hand to her back and lick over her glistening pussy, tracing a line up to the little rosette of her asshole.

She moans when I swirl my tongue inside her, and I wonder if I should take her there. I bet she's never had a cock inside her ass.

I'll go as far as betting that she's probably never thought of it.

I start talking in Italian, telling her I want to fuck every hole in her body. Since she doesn't understand a fucking word I'm saying, I tell the truth with words I know would scare her. It's too raw and dirty for people who just met.

"What are you saying?" she moans, turning to look back at me, her hair falling over her face.

I smile back at her and run my fingers over the milky flesh of her ass.

"I just love your body, woman."

She looks surprised. A woman like this shouldn't be surprised to hear anyone say that. It enrages me once more because it's clear she looks that way because of her ex-husband.

That's fine. I'll fix that. His loss is my fucking gain. If he didn't lose her, there'd be no way I had ever ended up with her in my arms.

I grip her hips, and she turns away just as I slam into her and start owning her body again.

I pound into her tight cunt hard, and she grips the sheet moaning and arching her back. It's a beautiful sight.

She is a beautiful sight.

I take full advantage of her hungry body that's been starved for attention and give her the good pounding she needs, branding her insides with my cock.

The same way I won't forget her, she won't forget me either. Few women ever do. When they claim to, I know it's a lie they're telling themselves because they know not to expect anything from me but a good time.

I unleash on her body, and she screams. It's a sound I want to capture and keep forever. The sound is brimming with the pleasure I'm giving her. It fills the room and joins the erotic melody of our flesh slapping against each other.

"Nick!" she screams again, but the sound of my name on her gorgeous lips makes me lose grasp of my control completely, and I come so hard I fear the condom might burst.

My release flows from me into her hot passage, and I

almost regret the barrier stopping my seed from flowing into her.

I pull out of her, and she collapses into a heap against the sheet with her hair stuck to the glistening sweat on her back and chest.

I slip off the bed and take care of the condom in the bathroom, noticing my tousled hair and glowing skin in the mirror as I walk by. I look like I had wild sex.

When I head back out to the room and see the beauty lying on the bed, I take note that she looks the same.

It's fucking midnight, and I'm not done with that pussy yet. She gives me a shy smile when I get on the bed and lie next to her, scooping her into my arms.

"You look like you want me to fuck you again," I tease.

"Maybe I do."

"Maybe?" I nuzzle my face between the crook of her neck and her shoulder, making her laugh. "That doesn't sound convincing. Either you want me to fuck you again or not, goddess."

"I want you to."

"Say it." I want to hear the dirty words coming out of her mouth in that sexy Southern accent. "Say the words, sweet Tennessee."

Her cheeks color fiercely, and the elegant flush races down her body. "I want you to fuck me."

"Anytime, Bellezza."

She laughs louder when I scoop her up and carry her out onto the balcony into the hot tub.

It takes next to no time for me to get hard again, and that's where I take her once more.

When we return to the room, I fall asleep balls deep in her and wake before sunrise.

The clock on the wall says it's five in the morning.

Tennessee is fast asleep in my arms with her head resting against my chest and her magnolia scent imprinted on me.

It's time to go. I need to get my ass back to L.A. and back to the drawing board.

Everyone is eager to find Federico, and I don't want to look like the guy who can't fill his shoes.

If I'm honest, I don't want to seem like I can't fill my father's shoes either. His death and my family's continue to haunt me, and this thing with Federico is starting to remind me of that time.

Both Antonio and my family were killed because of personal vendettas.

This is as much a revenge kill as it is precautionary because if Federico can infiltrate and kill anyone associated with the D'Agostino name, it means he's not as scared of them as he should be.

This mission is just tricky because Federico is a clever motherfucker with the right connections to keep him hidden.

I will find him, though. Rest assured his days in the world of the living are numbered.

Tennessee stirs in my arms but doesn't wake.

I move to slip away from her, but she mindlessly presses her hand to my chest, and it holds me there.

For a moment, I allow myself to think about what her life must be or was like. And I don't want to go.

A few more hours won't hurt, will they?

I can issue my orders to Leo, and we can catch up later.

Running my finger down the side of her face, I take in

her beauty and remember all I did with this good girl last night.

I'm going to need more than just a few hours with her before I say goodbye. You don't spend a night like we had together and wrap it up a few hours later.

I'm not ready to leave her yet. I still want more. I just hope I can say goodbye when the time comes, because she's the kind of girl you keep and make yours.

After only one night, she feels like she belongs to me.

That's a hard bond to break.

Chapter Six

Tennessee

My mind awakens at the scent of him when I turn onto my side.

That musky scent of sandalwood and his masculine power is mixed in with the fresh smell of the sheets. It fills every inch of my body, arousing me all over again.

My eyes flutter open, and the instant I see my little dress in a heap on the plush cream carpet, I remember everything we did last night.

The raw erotic memory makes me sit up and look around the bedroom of the

very expensive suite I slept in last night. We came straight up here from the lounge.

The bedroom is separate from the rest of the suite, like an apartment. A classy, exquisite apartment.

Of course, I was completely blown away because the

place looks like where royalty would stay. The entire hotel is like that. I swear when the girls and I arrived, I even saw a few low-key celebs mulling around. That feels like it happened years ago.

Now I'm here, and last night, I slept with a stranger who breathed new life into my tired body and made me ache in ways I'd never felt before.

How the hell is it possible to be married to one person for fourteen years and be with someone else for one night and feel like this?

This—as if it's the first time I've been touched properly. The way a woman aches for a man's touch.

My mouth waters, but I instantly curb the craving because there's no way he's still here.

Right?

A man like Nick would have long gone before I woke because there are no expectations.

In my head, I sound like I'm taking this surprisingly well. Maybe it's because I have to. I've more than learned my lesson when it comes to men and expectations. If you can't expect your husband to keep his dick in his pants when it comes to your best friend, what can you expect of them?

Anything and everything—*or nothing.*

Nick probably moved on to the next hot thing to catch his attention.

If so... what's that noise in the living room?

My lips part when I consider the possibility that he could still be here.

Why would he be here, though?

It's morning, and from the look of the sun outside, it must be quite late. I glance at the clock on the wall and confirm I'm right. It's eight thirty.

Sliding off the bed, I decide to investigate. I wrap the sheet around my body,

then pad out into the living room, where I find Nick sitting shirtless by the window bay smoking a cigar as he thumbs through a wad of documents.

While shock suffuses my being that he's still here, he lifts his head and stares back at me.

I focus on those dark magnetic eyes of his and allow my gaze to scan over the Lord's Prayer tattooed over his biceps and torso. I'm not sure if it makes him look more sexy or scary, or both.

I didn't get the chance to get a good look at him last night. I was too busy being swept off the face of the earth to really give appreciation to the artwork.

I'm looking now, and if he's real and not some figment of my imagination, then my God, he's even more gorgeous in the radiant sunlight than he was last night.

And all I'm doing is staring. Like some loser.

"Hi... I... think I overslept." My voice sounds breathy, like I've just run a marathon. "And..."

He puts out the cigar and stands. Whatever I was going to say next dissipates from my mind when my eyes drop to the bulge of his cock pressing against his pants.

Nick marches up to me and steals my mind away with the same numbing kiss he fed me last night.

He doesn't say anything; he just feasts on my mouth and picks me up as if I'm weightless and carries me back to bed.

In the back of my mind, I remember the oh-so-important

fact that the girls and I are supposed to leave today. My plane leaves in a little over two hours.

"My flight is after lunch," I stutter as he sucks my breasts.

I moan from the luxuriating feel of his tongue swirling around my nipples, tasting me.

"Fuck it. I'll book you another one."

"What?"

"Just shut up and let me fuck you."

This is crazy, but the kind of crazy I can't fight. He parts my legs, lines his cock up with my entrance, and plunges deep inside me, claiming me again.

* * *

We don't leave the bed for pretty much the whole day, and he doesn't leave my body. It gets dark, and I think we drag ourselves away from each other because he has to leave.

I don't think there was another reason, or I'd still be beneath him in that bed.

At nine p.m., he helps me get my stuff from my room and takes me down to the lobby to see me off. I'm booked on the eleven-o'clock flight. The last plane leaving for to Charlotte tonight.

As I look at him, I can't believe I'm not going to see him again.

We stare at each other, and it comes to that natural pause where things should end, but I don't want to let go.

"You didn't have to pay for my flight," I say with a little smile, recalling how he insisted on paying because he kept me with him all day.

"Bellezza, I can't help it. I'm the kind of man who takes care of his woman." He takes my hand and plants a kiss on my knuckles while keeping his eyes on me.

I giggle like a schoolgirl, and I can feel my body blushing, too.

"That's good to know, and thanks."

"Anything for you."

I gaze back at him and stare deep into his eyes at the maddening cacophony of emotion. There's so much in there, I can't quite figure him out. However, what gets me every time I look at him is that spark. It lurks and peeks as if it's waiting to emerge from the corner it's hiding in.

"You're just..." My voice trails off as I stop myself from telling him I find him fascinating. It's too forward, and this is the end. There's no point.

"What?" He presses is luscious lips together.

"Different," I decide to say, almost sounding dreamingly. My stomach does a little flutter when his smile widens.

"I am different. But... not different in a good way."

"Why would you say that?"

"Because it's true." His dark eyes take me in with contemplation. "I don't think you'd like me that much if you knew how different I was."

Danger—I sense it. That's what he means, and it should terrify me, yet part of me craves it in him because I'm the moth drawn to a flame.

I also can't imagine not liking every aspect of a man who could treat me so well.

"I don't believe that." I borrow his words from last night, and he brushes his thumb over my cheek.

"My number is in your phone."

"Is it?"

"Yeah. If you're in L.A., let me know."

"I will, and if you're in North Carolina, let me know. I make the best cookies."

He laughs, revealing his pearly white teeth.

"Goddess, if I'm in North Carolina, I'm getting more than cookies from you."

"That works, too."

He leans forward and kisses me, and it feels like a kiss goodbye. As in forever.

Despite what we just said, I don't think I'm ever going to see him again, so it's time to step away from the fantasy, and the man, and get back to my life.

"Goodbye, Nick."

"Goodbye, sweet Tennessee."

I walk away and look back once over my shoulder before I head through the revolving doors.

He's still there and didn't walk off like I thought he would.

One quick wave, and I step outside into the crisp night air.

There are taxis already waiting outside, so I just jump into the first one and call Georgia as I pull away from the Marchesi.

She screams when she answers the phone, and the taxi driver glances back at me.

"Oh, my gosh, you need to tell me everything!" she screeches.

"Are you home?" I ask, distracting from the question.

"Yes, woman, I'm home, and I'm fine. I want to hear about you, though. Tell me Nick was amazing."

"He was amazing." He was amazing, yet here I am, driving away from him.

"What did you do? Did he take you out?"

"Um... no. We just stayed in."

She screams again, and this could be fifteen years ago when we were sixteen and in high school.

"Tennessee, you slut. Please tell me you enjoyed every inch of that man."

"I did."

"What's next?"

"Nothing," I answer a little too quickly. "Nothing's next. It was a good weekend, and I feel better."

She's quiet for a few seconds; then I hear her sigh.

"Alright, cousin. I'll see you in a little while. The girls are going to head up here for your birthday. They said to call them when you can."

"I will." I miss them already. It's been years since we've been without each other, but it's time for a change. "Speak to you later."

"Be safe."

We hang up, and I place my phone back in my back pocket. I gaze out the window and slip back into the shoes of the uncertain woman I was days ago.

I'd bet Georgia would have no trouble starting over if she were me. She was always the strongest and boldest of the two of us.

Like Aunt Grace-Ann, her mama, Georgia got away from the country life and headed for the big city to live out her dreams of working for herself.

I should have gone with her, but I did everything to please my mother.

So, when Mama found out I was pregnant and said I had to marry Kurt, I did.

She was never going to have a daughter living her life as a single parent the way Aunt Grace-Ann did when she had Georgia.

If I hadn't married Kurt and chosen the single parent route, it would have made her look bad.

After all, at the time, Mama was the new preacher's wife with a reputation to live up to. She would have damned me herself if I damaged her reputation by looking like some Jezebel.

To her, it was so much the better that Kurt was in love with me. I think he genuinely was and maybe still is. His parents also adored me, which is a huge part of why he wants me back.

As we approach the airport, I reach into my bag to check I have the right cash for the driver. That's when I notice I don't have my purse.

"Oh, God," I rasp out, trying to backtrack when I last saw it.

I had it when I was packing my things.

No, it was before that. I was still in Nick's room.

I must have left it there.

I tap on the driver's seat to get his attention. "I'm so sorry. I left my purse back at the hotel. Can we turn around, please?"

"Of course. Will you still be able to make your flight?"

"Yes, I'm early, and I shouldn't take too long in the hotel."

Unless I see Nick again.

I could call him and ask if he's seen my purse, but I don't

want to be the weird woman and call so soon after getting his number. He might regret giving it to me.

He's probably already left, too.

But... if not, and I do see him when I get there, that might be nice.

Chapter Seven

Nick

"Massimo, I'm going to head to L.A. in a little while," I say into my phone, balancing it between my shoulder and ear as I pack my things. "My flight is in two hours. I just have a few more things to wrap up."

Tennessee left her purse here. I'm going to see if there's anything with her address inside and send it to her.

I set it down on the coffee table and walk into the bedroom to gather the rest of my stuff.

"That's fine," he replies in that stern voice he's known for. "Check in once you get back. I want everyone on this. It's gone on for far too long."

"Agreed, boss. Just give me a little more time, and I'll eliminate the threat."

"Alright, Nick. Just get it done."

He hangs up, and I curse myself. This shit has gone on long enough, and something still feels off.

I open the wardrobe door, and out comes one mean-looking motherfucker with a long-reach knife.

I jump back just in time to stop him from slicing my throat. A good look at him, and I realize I recognize the fucker. This is Mario, Federico's younger brother.

"Fucking vermin," he wails, pulling out his gun.

"We'll fucking see which of us is vermin." I send a kick to his midsection, and he goes flying back into the mirrors. One of them shatters.

He falls on the ground, but it doesn't faze him.

Cocking the hammer on the gun, he tries to shoot me, but I jump out of the way and pull my gun.

When he tries to shoot me again, I shoot him right in his chest, but he still comes for me.

Summoning my inner beast, I launch myself at him, knocking him back to the floor. He drops his gun, and I grab his knife.

I like knives; they leave a mess, and you know the person on the other end of the blade suffered the intended pain that you dealt them. This motherfucker will get his end, but not before I interrogate him.

I grab his hair and hold the knife to his neck, ready to slice him.

He tries to fight me but only ends up cutting his skin on the blade.

"Where's Federico?" I demand.

"Fuck you. You think I'm telling you shit? You think you're so hot because you work for the D'Agostinos."

I stick the knife deeper into his skin, and he yelps.

"Tell me where he is or die."

"You're gonna have to kill me because I'm not telling you shit. You and yours will all get what's coming to you." He laughs. "The same way your daddy dearest went."

Before he can take his next breath, I slice his throat. Clearly, he was on a suicide mission if he can talk about my father.

He would have known that meant instant death.

Blood pours from his body as I rip into his veins, and as I lift my head, I see her—Tennessee—standing in the doorway with her purse in her hand, watching me.

Watching me kill a man.

The blood has drained from her skin, and her eyes are so wide, I fear they might swallow the rest of her face.

Blood is all over me. On my chest, my face, my hands.

"Tennessee—"

"Get away from me! Please—" Her voice cuts, and she backs away.

I rush after her, but she runs in the opposite direction, terrified of me.

This has to be irony at its finest. Not even half an hour ago, I told her she wouldn't like the real me, and she just got a taste of who I am.

She runs out of the room, and I follow.

But just as I round the corner, a bullet whizzes past my ear.

Fuck, that nearly hit me. I jump behind a column just as my attacker is about to fire again, and I end him before he can cock the hammer.

Glancing back down the hallway, I see no sign of Tennessee.

She got away. I let her get away. But what was I going to do? Hurt her to keep her quiet?

Fuck no.

I have to do something. I just slipped up in a big way, and there's no telling what she'll do.

Chapter Eight

Tennessee

Oh my God, my God, my God, my God.

I run as fast as my legs can carry me, adrenaline fueling my every move.

What the hell did I just witness?

I couldn't have seen what I just saw, right?

Nick...

He just killed a man.

Nick, the man I spent last night with and all of today, killed a man.

He just... held a knife to the man's neck and sliced the blade right across as if he were cutting through a piece of meat. And he didn't cut him clean either.

Nick was like a savage. He almost hacked the man's head off. That's why all the blood came rushing out of the man's body the way it did.

God, there was so much blood, and I heard bullets. It

was like I just walked onto the set of some crazy action film, right in the middle of a gun battle.

When I first arrived at the suite, I assumed the maids were inside, because I could open the door without a keycard.

I went in and saw my purse on the table in the living room, so I picked it up. That's when I heard Nick's voice in the bedroom, followed by a noise that sounded like he was fighting with someone.

The gunshot was what I heard next, and I only went to the room because I knew he was in there. If not, I would have run the moment I heard the gun go off.

I can't even believe I'm thinking the word 'gun.' Where I come from, the only people I know who carry them are the police or people who work with them.

Bree's husband, Ethan, is a detective, and Quinn's husband, Logan, is a private investigator. They carry guns, but I've never seen either of them with one.

Yet tonight, I witnessed a murder.

By the time I got to the room, I didn't know who had the gun. It was clear, though, from what Nick said to the man, that he had control. He didn't seem to be defending himself or anything like that.

He killed him, and I saw, and he knows that I saw.

I jump into the taxi that is waiting for me and tell the driver to go.

I'm breathing so hard I can't steady my racing heart.

"Are you okay, Miss?" the driver asks, glancing back at me.

I open my mouth to answer, but I stop because I don't know what I'm supposed to say.

No, I'm not okay. I just witnessed a murder, and the killer saw me.

What's going to happen to me now?

Nick knows my name. He knows I'm going to North Carolina, and he knows personal things about me.

I barely got away. I heard more gun fire, but I didn't look back to see what was happening.

I don't even know if he got shot. If he didn't, then I don't believe for one second he's just going to let me go.

What do I do now?

Where do I go?

Shit.

Chapter Nine

Nick

"Fuck, damn it."

She's gone. I rush out to the lobby, unable to find her anywhere.

Did I seriously expect her to stick around?

She probably got into the first taxi and hightailed it out of here.

Shit.

What the fuck do I do now?

People are looking at me as I make my way through the area and walk outside the building. I look up and down the road, but there really is no point.

If I could have talked to her, I would have been able to explain what happened. That's if she listened to me.

And I'm making things worse. Right now, I have two dead bodies upstairs that I can't just leave there.

I call the concierge to tell him to keep people away from the tenth floor, then I call the clean-up crew.

* * *

"They were waiting for you," Leo states, looking over Mario's dead body.

We're at the vet the cleanup crew uses to dispose of bodies. I wanted to check out Mario first before we roast him. The other guy didn't have anything on him, and it's not looking like Mario had anything either.

"Which means they were watching me," I answer.

Leo dips his head, and his messy hair falls over his eyes. "They were fucking watching you, and they wanted to take you out."

I knew something was off. This was it. I fell into my own trap.

I've just reported to Massimo, and of course, I haven't told either him or Leo about Tennessee.

As far as either of them are concerned, she doesn't exist.

While I can maybe contain things at the hotel, I can't control what she does outside it. Like if she goes to the cops.

One mention of my name, and it won't just be cops involved. It would be feds, too. Maybe even more than that.

The worst thing for anyone in the mafia is to have cops crawling all over your ass. If cops start asking questions, that will get back to the hotel, and they're not going to like that either. It shakes the foundation of what we in the underground keep secret.

"What now?" Leo asks.

"We need more eyes. It wouldn't have just been two of

them. Go back to the hotel and question security. See what you can find out."

"Sure." He nods and leaves.

I instruct the vet to deal with Mario, and I head the other way.

I have another place I stay at here when I can't make it to the hotel. Since two people tried to kill me tonight, I think it's best I head there and reconvene.

I need to find out where Tennessee lives and talk to her.

That's what I need to focus on now. Once that's done, I'll hopefully be able to get back on track to finding Federico.

All the time I was with Tennessee, I never wanted her to see my darkness.

I knew she'd never want to be with me if she knew I killed for a living.

Mostly, I didn't want her to do what she did— take one look at me and run the other way.

My phone rings in my back pocket, and I reach for it believing it's Leo or Massimo. It's neither. The call is coming from an unrecognized number.

"Who is this?" I say, stopping in the foyer.

"Heard you were looking for me," comes a cold hard voice.

I've never heard the voice before, but my gut tells me who it belongs to.

"I look for a lot of people in my line of work."

He chuckles without humor. "I'm sure you do, Nick Bellotto, but you've been looking for me for quite some time now. This is Federico DiMaggio. I already wanted you dead, but now that you've killed my little brother, you have to pay with more than your life."

"My, my, don't we have one rule for one and another for others. Your fucking brother came to kill me."

Fucking asshole. It's bold of him to call me. The fucking call also confirms his lack of care for who I am.

That's why I don't underestimate his threats.

He's not going to call someone like me unless he has something to hold over my head.

"That was a pretty red-haired girl you had hanging on your arm, Nicky."

Something to hang over my head like that. My heart stills and fucking stops in my chest.

Tennessee. He's talking about her. Talking about her as if he saw her. Like he was here in Vegas at the Marchesi just like we were told.

Fuck.

"Big tits, bubble ass, fine body, beautiful red hair, heart-melting smile," he taunts. "Oh, the way she looked at you was to die for. Like you were her everything."

"You leave her out of this."

"Let me guess, weekend away in Vegas with your girlfriend. Maybe you thought you could kill two birds with one stone. Kill me and get some pussy at the same time," he intones in a sing-song voice that grates on my nerves.

"Where are you going with this, you asshole?" I need to know what he's planning.

"Her. She's your price. I will kill her. I'll take her blood for my brother's. I'll watch you suffer from the loss of your love, then I'll kill you next."

Shock slams through me, and before I can answer, he hangs up.

I'm left staring into space, my pulse galloping, my mind going crazy.

Being with me put Tennessee in danger. As if things weren't fucking bad enough.

Federico is going to find her and kill her.

I can't allow that to happen. So, I have to find her first.

She felt like mine, so she is. She's mine.

Mine to protect.

Mine to keep safe.

Chapter Ten

Tennessee

I'm a nervous wreck.

A complete mess inside and out. I've been sitting in the kitchen with Georgia trying to force a sandwich down my throat.

Georgia has been talking non-stop for the last hour. She was like that this morning, too, when she picked me up from the airport. My flight was a little under five hours long. I love catching up on sleep on long flights, but I was so shaken up, sleep was the furthest thing from me.

By the time I saw Georgia, I was an exhausted mess, and all she wanted to do was talk about Nick. When she saw I wasn't saying any more about him than I had, she began talking about this new business venture of ours. I was glad for the subject change, but it wasn't the sort of thing I wanted to talk about at three in the morning.

She's talking about it again now, and it's nearly four in the afternoon.

I managed to sleep for a few hours, but my mood isn't any better.

I'm just humoring her because I know she's excited. The business finally has a chance to be successful. I can see how my presence will take it to the next level. The simple advert I ran last week when I first arrived grabbed us an amazing contract with a nice four-figure sum to provide the cake and catering for a wedding at the end of next month.

While she's been talking at the speed of light, I've been sitting here too numb to breathe as I mulled over all the conversations I had with Nick. I've been trying to think of anything I said to him that would allow him to find me.

I was so freaked out last night, I wasn't even sure I should come home. I worried I'd put Georgia in danger. I'm only here because I convinced myself that I didn't tell Nick enough information to find me.

Even if he looked through my purse, there wasn't anything in there with my address on it. My driver's license and passport were already in the bag I was carrying.

I didn't tell Nick where I worked or anything like that. I also left my phone in the bathroom in the airport in Vegas on purpose.

I've seen enough films to know you can be tracked through your cellphone. If he was able to get into my phone and put his number in, it means he also had my number. Even if he doesn't, I didn't want to take the risk, so I wrote down all the numbers I'd need and ditched the phone.

Other than that, I don't think he'll be able to track me down.

I'm currently staying with Georgia until I buy my own house. The business is also listed in Georgia's name, and he doesn't know her name.

We're finalizing the contracts this week, but I think I'll hold off on that for a while.

Thank God Nick and I didn't do much talking. Who knows what I could have said?

I trusted him. Trusted him foolishly with my body, and in some ways, my heart.

I don't even know how that happened, and I don't think it's been down to desperation. I'm not a desperate woman who needed to go to Vegas to be fucked by some random stranger.

It's more the case of hurt.

I hate Kurt for what he did to me, but more than anything, he hurt me.

Since the whole thing with him, I've been like an open book. Sometimes, my heart is so full I'm ready to pour out my emotions to whoever will listen.

That's what happens sometimes when you've been wronged. Either you want to shout it from the rooftop, or you go the other way and don't talk.

I can't expect this plan to hide to last forever. It's only until I can figure out what to do and how to keep myself safe.

Also... I saw a man die.

How do I keep quiet about that?

It goes against my morals to even think I can forget what I saw.

I need to go to the police and report the crime, but I need to do it in a way that doesn't track back to me.

While I want to do what's right, I don't want to put my

face out there to be some kind of hero and end up getting backlash for it. Or die."

That could happen, and it might not be Nick who kills me.

Clearly, that man wasn't exactly a saint either. I heard his threats and what he said about Nick's father. He made it sound like he had other people who would come.

Nick snapped after that.

Shit. I shouldn't have gotten involved with him. I should have listened to my gut and turned him down at the table before he could even open his mouth.

I've been through so much. Things are already bad as it is and unsteady in my life.

Even before Kurt screwed with me, I had Mama, and I still have her breathing down my neck to take him back. She actually told me he was the best thing to happen to me, and it was my fault he cheated.

Eight months ago, when I walked in on Mary riding his cock in his office, it was confirmation to my heart that he was the worst thing to happen to me.

Last Friday, when the divorce papers came through, mere days before I was scheduled to leave Wilmington, Kurt came to the house to cause a scene. He didn't know I was leaving town, and since I got to keep the house in the divorce settlement, he thought that's where I was going to keep living.

Georgia grabs my hand, making me jump. I almost fall off my chair.

"What is with you?" she giggles. "You've been spaced out since you got back."

I release a haggard sigh. "Sorry, I think I'm tired."

She gives me a saucy smile. "Of course, you would be, after the weekend you had."

"You're not going to let me forget about that anytime soon, are you?" I try to sound normal, but there's a slight quiver in my voice.

"Nope. It's so much the better that it happened to you. Can you imagine what your mama would say if she ever found out?" She gives me her best villain laugh.

It makes me smile. I actually can't think of what my mother would do. She'd probably fly me over to the Pope himself and get him to dip me in the Red Sea to cleanse my sins.

"Well, I know she wouldn't just have a fit."

"No, ma'am, she would not. Have you heard from her?"

"Of course, I have. She's been calling, but I don't answer the phone." The same phone I left in Vegas. I'll at least wait a week before I get a new phone and number.

"Maybe silence is best for a while."

"I know it is."

"Alrighty, Miss Lady, we've got work to do. I'm going to town to see that new boutique I wanted to order those cupcake holders from."

"Is it okay if I work from home today? I mean, if the girls are in and everything can run without me."

She nods. "Yes, absolutely. After the magic you worked last week, you can do anything you want."

I wouldn't call it magic. I'm just good with business. I took some community college classes in marketing and advertising. I always wanted my own business, and Georgia and I always had a knack for cooking and baking. We did the catering for all sorts of things back home and always talked about going into business together.

This was perfect. She had everything set up, and I just came along and became an addition.

"Thanks, Cuz."

"You okay?" Her eyes fill with concern.

"I'm fine. I will be fine."

"Alright. I'll see you later. I'll be back late tonight, but call me if you need anything."

"Sure."

She saunters away, and I return my gaze to the glass panels on the kitchen window.

I think the best thing to do is to go to town and use one of the public phones to call the police. I could park my car outside town, then walk the rest of the way. That way, if they try to track me, I'd hopefully throw them off.

I down the rest of my coffee, which now tastes as bitter as gone-off licorice, and stand. It's time to do something more than think. The sooner I can get this over and done with, the quicker I can get back to starting over.

Making my way into the hallway to grab my jacket, I do a mental check of what I need to do.

The moment I grab my jacket from the coat holder, Nick steps out of the living room, and my heart stops beating.

My God, he found me.

I was wrong. I gave him just the right amount of information to find me.

Now he's here.

Chapter Eleven

Tennessee

"Tennessee, we need to talk," he says in a tentative voice that doesn't suit his alpha personality.

What do I know, though?

The only thing I know about him is that he's a killer.

My body is so numb I can't get it to do anything. It's as if I've stopped working and all my vital organs are shutting down.

I will my body to do anything besides stand here and look at the man who's clearly flown across the country to kill me, but not even the flight response a person would normally get in a situation like this is working for me.

Maybe because it's impaired just like everything else inside me. When I look at him, I want to see him as the killer I saw in Vegas, but what I see is the fantasy, and I remember how he made me feel.

"Tennessee." He comes closer and touches my cheek.

That does it. The mere touch jolts my body like a spark plug awakening a dead battery in a car.

My brain snaps into focus, and I step away.

When I look at him now, I remember how he killed that man and chased after me when I ran away.

He's here. What happened in Vegas followed me home, and I feel like I should have known he was the devil when he first smiled at me. Not just a dangerous man.

Evil.

"Baby, it's important you listen to me."

"*Listen?*" I can barely say the word. "Please, just leave me alone. Don't hurt me. I won't tell anyone what I saw."

What a hypocrite I am. I was just going out the door to report him to the police.

"Tennessee, you need to come with me. You're in danger."

"Yes, I am in danger. From you. I saw what you did to that man."

"He came to kill me. Please, just come with me, and we'll talk properly when I get you somewhere safe." He reaches for me, but I back into the wall.

"Don't touch me."

I stumble over my feet when I retreat to the kitchen.

He comes after me, and I run to the back door, my heart galloping in my chest so fast I fear it might leap out and keep running.

I manage to open the door and run out into the garden. There I crash into a monstrous man who looks like the Hulk, and he grabs me.

I scream as he hoists me off the ground and places a gun

to the side of my head. The *click-clack* of the hammer sounds in my ear along with the fire of the gun.

I expect to be dead, but I'm still aware of what's happening when I find myself falling.

The hulking man drops to the ground next to me with a bullet hole in his forehead, and I whip around to see Nick standing across from me holding out his gun.

It was him who shot the man.

I assumed he was with Nick, but he wasn't. That man would have killed me just now.

So, I am in danger?

Tears track down my cheeks, but I don't get the moment to sink into despair and allow the shock of what's happening to consume me.

A loud crash slams into the fence, and the side door flies open. Four men rush in carrying guns.

Nick rushes to my side seconds before they open fire. He scoops me up and covers me with his body while he shoots back at the men.

He gets me back inside the house, then out the front door, where he takes my hand and we run down the street.

The men are behind us, coming to get us. Coming to kill us.

With my heart in my throat, I run as fast as I can, pushing my body to move for survival.

Jesus, I can't believe this is happening to me.

I didn't do anything wrong. I don't even know who these people are, but they're here to kill me.

And the man I was running from is the one who's helping me escape.

When we reach a black SUV at the end of the curb, he yanks the door open and lifts me into the passenger seat.

Frantically, I look back at the men pursuing us while he gets into the car and drives.

The men get in their cars and follow us.

Nick accelerates as we turn onto the road, but I already know we won't be able to get away easily.

There are too many of them.

We drive until we blend in with other cars heading into the town. Then we see the lever crossing coming down as an oncoming train approaches. To my horror, Nick keeps going and doesn't stop.

I scream as we drive onto the tracks, and the sound of the train raises every nerve in my body.

We just make it across, and I pray with everything inside me we're safe now.

My hope extinguishes, however, when I look back and see one of the cars still tailing us. The others got left behind at the crossing.

"Fuck. Hold on tight!" Nick shouts.

He speeds up, driving way past the speed limit for this area, and we race across the grass, cutting through the walkway leading up to the town library. That takes us to the highway, where the prick continues to follow.

I can't believe this is really happening, and there's not a damn thing I can do besides sit here in this car and allow Nick to take me to wherever he's taking me.

When we get onto the country roads, the traffic thins. Soon, we become the only two cars on the road. The asshole takes that opportunity to shoot at us.

"Take the wheel and keep it steady," Nick orders

Summoning bravery, I grab the steering wheel while he takes out his gun and leans out the window to shoot back at the man.

Gunfire explodes all around me like a warzone, and the car gets hit multiple times. The back wheel on my left blows out, and the windows shatter.

Something explodes, and I lose control of the car. Nothing works.

Just before we go over the side of the road and into the ditch, I notice the other car following us, except the man inside is already dead.

When Nick and I land, the airbags automatically engage, blasting me back into the seat as we smash into a thicket of trees.

* * *

"Tennessee," Nick says, but he sounds like he's far, far away.

My eyes are closed. When I open them, I see his face looming before me. There's a nasty gash over his eye and blood streaming down the side of his face.

I try to sit up, but my body feels shaken. Then I remember what happened.

Judging from the way Nick looks and everything else, I think I must have blacked out for a moment.

"Are you okay?" he asks, and I hand him back an incredulous glare.

"No. Of course I'm not okay."

"Are you hurt?"

"I feel shaken."

"That's good enough for me. We have to get out of here."

"Why is this happening?" I ask him in a croaking voice.

"Tennessee, we can't stop to talk. We don't know how far behind the others could be, and my phone's broken. We're on our own until I can get to a phone."

"I need to know why these people are after me," I insist.

"And I need to keep you safe. Let's go."

He grabs me before I can protest, and we climb out of the wreck through his side.

We walk over to the other car, and I can confirm if the man inside wasn't dead when I saw him, the tree branch spearing his body like a skewer definitely killed him.

I bring my hands up to my cheeks and gasp at the horrific sight.

Nick, on the other hand, releases me to yank open the car door and starts searching the man. He takes the man's gun and starts cursing in Italian.

"No fucking phone. Fucking asshole." Nick spits on the man's face and slams the door back shut.

A feral look enters his eyes when he faces me and takes my hand.

I feel afraid of him again. Not scared enough, however, to stop me from asking the questions I need answers to.

"Why is this happening to me?" I ask again as we start walking through the woods.

He glances back at me and clenches his jaw. "Because of me."

"What do you mean?" I glare back at him. "That makes no sense."

"They think we're a couple."

My blood spikes from this news. "But we aren't. I never even knew you existed until days ago."

"They don't care about that. The man you saw me kill is the brother of someone I'm looking for. He wants you dead because he thinks you're my girl."

My gaze rivets to his, and I find I can't look away. Maybe it was the way he said *my girl*.

But I'm not, though. I'm nobody's girl. I'll take care of myself from now on.

"Didn't you tell him he made a mistake?"

"Bellezza, that's not how it works."

Calling me Bellezza conjures memories I don't want of him, so I force them away.

"How does it work, then?"

"Death is all we know."

"Who is *we*?" That sounded like they're all the same. And like there could be more of them. He also mentioned that we were on our own now. I wasn't aware that wasn't the case before. That aside, more and more I'm starting to see he can't be who he says he is. "You aren't a consultant, are you? How did you even find me? How did they?" The questions tumble mindlessly from my lips.

He gives me an uneasy look. "It's best you don't know the answers to any of those questions."

"Tell me now. This is your fault. I didn't ask for this."

He glares at me, and his eyes darken. "I'm an enforcer in the mafia. I kill people for a living, and sometimes they get back at me. That's what's happening now, Bellezza. They think you're mine. And I'm here because you are."

Chapter Twelve

Nick

Everything that could go wrong has gone to shit.

Fuck.

All I have are weapons, but they're not going to last.

The most I can hope for now is for us to get to safety and somewhere I can get help. If I were by myself, I wouldn't care about getting help.

I'd fight to the death like how all enforcers who work for the D'Agostinos are trained. That's how my father trained them.

He wanted us to be like Spartans, and that's what we became.

I have to be that for Tennessee now in other ways.

She's stopped resisting, which is good, but she's also stopped talking. I almost preferred it when she was scared of me, or angry. Now there's nothing, and we are in hell.

We've been walking through these woods for hours. It feels like we've been going around in circles, although I know we haven't. I have a good sense of direction. The problem is, wherever we are is far away from civilization.

We were far enough away in the first place; then we branched off into the wilderness. I was hoping the route we took would lead back to town, but it hasn't, and since I know those fuckers would have come after us, the priority is to get somewhere safe.

Once we do that, I can make other plans to get us out of this mess. Leo is here with me in Charlotte. I also called in some backup who would have arrived after us.

Of course, I had to tell Leo what happened with Tennessee. I didn't think it was wise to come here on my own. Little did I know alone is exactly how I'd end up.

I preempted Federico would have pretty much the same timeframe I had to find Tennessee. So, after I spoke to him, I got on the next plane to Charlotte and found Tennessee's details on the way. In la Costa Nostra, all we need is a name to find whatever we want on a person.

Within ten minutes of me landing, the phone call I got from D'Agostinos Inc. gave me everything I needed to know to find her and her cousin.

Because Tennessee isn't used to my kind of life, she wouldn't have known not to go home. I guessed she would have thought she was safe there because she never gave me an address. The clever little thing she was ditched her phone, though. That was a smart move, just not enough.

I don't know when Federico's guys got there, but I think they saw me slip into the house. I hid in the closet for at least an hour before Georgia left. I didn't want to cause a scene with Georgia there, and I think Federico's men were waiting for me to strike.

They knew once her cousin left, I'd make my move, and the goal was clearly to take us both out.

"We can't keep walking around like this," Tennessee says against the silence. Her voice sounds weary and raspy, as if she hasn't spoken in days.

"I know. We just need to get somewhere safe." I hope we find somewhere soon. Night's about to fall. Once it gets dark, being out here in the open woods will be as good as serving ourselves up to the enemy on a plate.

Besides, I don't know what kind of animals may be out here, and I don't want to waste the ammo.

Another half an hour passes, and we come across a dilapidated cottage with the roof caved in.

"Let's check in there," I say.

We head over there, and I'm almost afraid of what we'll find when we go in. The cottage looks like something from a horror film.

The door creaks open when I push it and almost falls off the hinges.

I allow Tennessee to go inside first, and I follow closely behind. The place looks like hell, and it's clear nobody's been in here for so long it carries that unlived-in smell and silence.

"The place must have been ruined in the hurricanes a few years back," Tennessee surmises, looking around.

A hurricane explains the devastation perfectly.

"Let's see what we can find." It's a long shot that I might find a radio or some way of communicating with the world outside the forest, but I try to have hope.

Of course, I find nothing, but at least there's a box of candles and water running from the taps in the kitchen. As I'm not sure how clean it is to drink, I'm going to try and find the water source or another one. There must be a river nearby.

"What now?" Tennessee asks, walking into the kitchen.

"We stay here and figure things out."

"We're going to stay here for the night?" She raises a brow.

"It's the best idea I have so far. Let's go down to the basement. It will be warmer." I don't want to stay here any more than she does, but it's a good place to be if trouble comes. We can take cover behind these walls, and I can protect her better.

I light one of the candles, and we make our way down into the dark, dank basement.

A moldy smell hits me when we reach the bottom of the stairs, and I look around to see boxes everywhere. I place the candle on the table in the middle of the room and find some old curtains on top of one of the boxes.

I lay them down on the floor for Tennessee to sit on.

"Come here. Sit and rest. I'm going to check the surrounding area a little better."

She sits and wraps the longer parts of the curtains around her shoulders to keep warm. Seeing how flimsy the fabric is, I take off my jacket and throw it around her, surprising her.

"Thank you," she mutters.

"Don't mention it."

"Will you be long?" Her hands tremble, and her skin looks paler.

"No. I won't go far either. Just stay here."

"Where else am I going to go?" She furrows her brows and gives me that pissed-off stare I first got hours ago when I told her this was happening because of me.

"I just don't want you getting any ideas."

"Believe me, I have none. I don't even know how to use a gun."

"I'll take care of you."

The pissed-off look swiftly morphs into that stunned expression she had when I told her she was mine.

"What if they find us?" Her breath hitches. "There were a lot of them."

"Let's worry about that if it happens." I turn to go back up the stairs, but she stops me.

"What happened to your father?" she asks.

"My father?" My nerves spike the way they always do whenever I have to talk about him.

"That guy back at the hotel said something about him."

"My family was murdered. My mother, sister, and father. When it came to my father, they made an example out of him."

Tennessee sucks in a breath, and her eyes widen. "I'm so sorry. I never thought it was that."

"It's okay."

It's not okay, but I always say that by default. When it comes to my family, it will never be okay, even though I killed the people responsible for taking them from me.

My mother and sister were shot in the head. It looked like they were killed execution style. My father had his eyes gouged out and his body mutilated.

I was surprised he was alive when I found him. All he

said to me is to never forget who I am and who he taught me to be.

Their deaths were a revenge kill. Father killed his enemy's wife by accident, and they came to kill us in return. They didn't come for me because they knew I would have ended them. They got to my father when he least expected it.

It happened eight years ago. I'd just turned twenty-six, and it was the worst time of my life.

"I'll be back," I promise, and she nods.

"Thanks—for coming for me."

"You don't have to thank me for that." I turn and go before I allow myself to get lost in her gaze.

Chapter Thirteen

Tennessee

It's dark now, and Nick's not back.

He's been gone for over an hour.

I'm terrified, and I'm worried about Georgia.

I worry those men will hurt her. I don't know what I'd do if that happened.

I feel like all I've brought on myself is problems—more of them.

The problems already existed in my life, but I had to go and make it worse by having a one-night stand with a man I just met and knew nothing about.

A shuffling noise sounds upstairs, and my poor heart stills. I hold my breath, then release it with relief when Nick walks down the stairs.

He's back, and he's carrying a bottle of water.

When I look at him, I don't see the killer. I'm seeing the

caring man who took care of me again. And I feel sad for his loss.

I can't imagine losing my family that way. I lost my father, too, but it was to a heart condition. He wasn't killed, and although I wish I'd had more years with him, I know I'd feel worse if I were Nick and had my family stolen from me.

"Drink this." He moves toward me and hands me the bottle of water.

"Thanks." When I take it and drink, I realize just how thirsty I am.

"Have these, too." He pulls out a little bag with some red berries inside. I take them and eat. "We're not that far from town, but it's a good walk. Our smartest option is to stay here until sunrise, then move when it's light. At the same time, we're not safe here."

The knots in my stomach tighten. "You think they're going to find us here?"

"I think they could. I'm just reluctant to keep going because it's dark. They have the advantage of numbers. If we get attacked out in the open, that's it. At least here, if they come for us, we stand a chance."

It all sounds bad to me, and then there's Georgia to consider. "I'm worried about my cousin."

"My people will have gone to the house and are watching the shop. They'll take care of her. I know they will."

"Are they... like you?" *More mafia men.* I'm almost afraid of the answer because of the connotations attached to the mafia.

"Yes, they are like me." He holds my gaze, and the amber

flame of the candle gives him an eerie glow. "So, I know she's in good hands."

I don't think we can know anything for certain, but at least knowing there are people around who can protect her gives me some hope. Even until morning.

"You still look like you're afraid of me," he adds, intensifying his gaze.

"Any reason I shouldn't be? I'm still a loose end, aren't I? I still saw you kill a man." It seems so silly to say now because I've seen two more dead men since.

"You did, and yes, you are a loose end."

"What are you going to do to me?" He could have allowed those men to kill me, and the problem would have been solved. Since he hasn't, I need to know his plans for me.

"Maybe I shouldn't answer that question." There's an unmistakable glimmer of lust in his gaze, which triggers my arousal all over again.

"Maybe you should."

He gives me a smile that can only be described as deliciously dark and full of wild unspoken sexual promises. I don't know how he can even smile at a time like this, but I suppose he must be used to being in danger.

He's a damn hitman, for crying out loud.

"Sweet, Tennessee, I don't think you want to hear the truly dirty thoughts riddling my mind."

"No, I don't." It's a lie. I know it's a damn lie because my traitorous body wants to hear everything. Following my body has nearly gotten me killed. So, I swallow to loosen the lust-filled lump swelling my throat and try to focus. "Nick, I need to know what you're going to do to me."

"I'm not going to hurt you. I'm not a complete monster."

He's not a good person either. "Does that mean you're going to let me go if we get out of this? Would you have let me go in Vegas?"

"You don't have to worry about me hurting you, sweet Tennessee. But I don't think I have to tell you that you need to keep quiet about everything you've seen me do. I haven't killed anyone who didn't try to kill me first. That man in Vegas was watching us the whole time and waiting for the moment to strike."

"Why did he want to kill you?" There are always two sides to a story.

"Because I'm looking to kill his brother, who killed a man who was like family to me."

Killing and violence. Those are the only concepts this man seems to know. Now that we're finally talking, I understand the danger I sensed in him when we first met.

But who am I to judge him when I don't know him or what his life must be like?

"When does the killing end?"

"Never, because darkness knows no good. Sometimes, death is the only way to keep people safe. Let's take our present situation as a good example. Did you think I could simply talk to the man holding you at gunpoint in your garden and ask him to let you go? Or tell the men chasing us to stop because you had nothing to do with me or my life before last weekend?"

There's only one answer to that. "No."

"Good, it looks like we're on the same page. Those men are hired to kill, and if they miss the mark, either they'll pay with their lives or someone they know will. They won't stop hunting until they hit their target. Understand better?"

"Yes... what happens after this?"

"I let you go either way, and it would be in your best interest to keep quiet. Can I have your word that you will?"

What choice do I have? "Yes. Won't people have questions, though, about the dead? I'm sure the police would have been notified."

"My people would have already taken care of that."

Bile suddenly churns my stomach, and I imagine those mobster movies where they bury bodies in the desert, or they find some other way of getting rid of you.

The clash of thoughts and emotions inside me peaks when Nick sits beside me. The scent of him, and the sudden closeness, makes it a million times harder to quell my arousal.

I'm so conflicted, and whether I like it or not, I'm still attracted to him.

Even if I tried not to be, my body would betray me. It still remembers the unimaginable pleasure he gave every inch of my being.

I'm getting wet now just thinking about it. That can't be normal. I wish I could say it was down to the situation not making me think straight, or even me just not being myself.

But it's neither of those. It's him, and I never expected to see him again. His presence in my world again has me twisted.

"What are you?" I hear myself say, and he returns his gaze to me.

"You know what I am."

"But you just said you're not a complete monster, so what are you, then?"

He smirks, and the sight of the mere smile sparks something inside me.

"I'm just a man. A bad one." He drags in a breath. "But maybe I still have a soul." He looks away and rests his head against the wall. "I'm sorry I brought this on you. I would have left you alone if I knew this could happen."

The rule-following, law-abiding realist in me wishes he had left me alone, but the glimmer of the person I used to be thinks of the time we had together.

That part of me would scarily choose to do the same thing all over again, even knowing the danger and the threat this man represents.

That part of me would still choose him because if he had left me alone, I would never know him.

I would have gone to Vegas with my friends and had the girly weekend we set out for. I would have fake smiled my way through, gone shopping, eaten, and gambled, then headed back to Charlotte to slip back into the shoes of the woman who'd been cheated on.

After being with Nick, it felt like he'd breathed new life into me, which means he meant more to me than a man you forget after a one-night stand.

He must be something more if he came to protect me and called me his.

That didn't escape me. I just haven't entertained the thought because it's nice, and a complete juxtaposition to the situation and us.

"I guess these things happen sometimes," I mutter.

"They shouldn't to women like you."

"Maybe not, but I have the worst luck ever, so something was bound to happen eventually."

He shuffles to face me. "I don't believe that, and I'm going to get you out of here and back to your family."

"That would be nice. At this point, I'd even be thrilled to see my mother. I'd even take the cussing she'd give me and the uppity looks of pity she and my stepfather always cast my way."

"You don't have a good relationship with your mother?"

I shake my head. "Never have."

"Why?"

I chuckle without humor. "It would take me a long time to answer that question."

"We have time."

"I doubt you'd want to use that time to listen to me talk about my mother, and my life."

"Try me."

Maybe talking about Mama might be a good distraction from the weird sexual vibe still sparking between us.

"My mother is one of those high society women who love money and prestige. She's a control freak who needs to have everything and everyone a certain way." That's a good summary. "She was the main reason I married Kurt—my ex."

"Your mother forced you to marry him?"

"Yes. I was pregnant, and he comes from a rich family. We were together in high school, but I never saw myself spending the rest of my life with him. My mother forced the wedding and the marriage on me. Months later, I lost the baby, and she blamed me. Years passed, and we found out I can't have kids. She blamed me for that, too." Every time I say that out loud, a piece of my soul dies.

Kurt's family wanted grandchildren, and so did Mama. In the years before everything fell apart, we tried everything under the sun to get me pregnant, but nothing worked. I had five miscarriages, several rounds of IVF, and that was it. The doctors declared me infertile, and my only options were adoption or a surrogate, but without my eggs.

I was willing. I thought it would be nice to adopt a child who needed a loving home, but Kurt didn't want to pursue either option. That's when the arguments began and maybe when Mary started fucking my husband.

"How can that be your fault?" Nick cuts into my thoughts.

"My mother found a way to blame me for everything, so she thought it was perfectly understandable that Kurt cheated on me. And since my ex-best friend already has kids, Mama thought it made even more sense. She called me an evil bitch when I wouldn't take him back. That's how I ended up leaving Wilmington and living with my cousin."

"Sounds like you made a wise choice."

"I think so."

"You think? You don't sound too certain."

"I am certain."

"Oh, because for a moment there, I thought you might be in two minds about your ex. Fourteen years is a long time to be with someone."

"I just want to forget him. Forget I ever met him and that we were ever together."

"Is that why you went to Vegas? To forget?" His eyes darken again to that magnetic color, lulling me to get lost in the attraction rippling between us.

It beckons me to give him the truth. "I didn't go to Vegas to forget, but I did forget him when I was with you."

I should regret the confession, but I don't. He reaches

forward and touches my cheek, then he catches my face, and suddenly I'm trapped.

The lump expands in my throat, and the silence filling the space between us feels like it's about to explode from the anticipation coming from me.

Before my next thought can take fruition, Nick leans in and kisses me. His lips crush mine and transport me back to the way we were in Vegas as I lay beneath him and he devoured me.

I want to feel that again.

"Stop me," he speaks against my lips.

"Why?"

"Because now you know I'm the devil. If you don't stop me, I will fuck you right here against this wall, and there will be nothing about me you'll want to forget."

"I don't want to forget you."

"Then you will get burned."

He reclaims my lips, and I slip my arms around his neck. He lifts me and pushes me against the wall.

Moments later, he's got my pants off and my panties sitting next to them, and he's unbuckling his belt to take out his cock.

I manage a sip of air, then he lifts my leg around him and plunges deep inside my pussy.

I bite back a moan, still mindful that we have to be quiet, but it becomes hard when he starts fucking me against the wall like he wants to own me again.

The skin-to-skin contact is unreal, and his lips on mine taste like sweet forbidden passion fueling this dark fantasy. I know it's everything that will burn me when this is over.

He drives into me deeper and faster and harder.

I come instantly and ride the waves of bliss coursing through me as he continues to pound into me.

I get lost in his maddening thrusts, my body weakening with pleasure yet still greedy for more. He gives it to me, and when I come again, he comes, too, filling me with his hot cum. The spray hits my G-spot, and I grip his powerful shoulders as my body shudders against his.

Held against him, I savor the rapid beat of his heart, and when he kisses me again, I savor him, knowing now for certain I'll never forget him.

That's what's going to burn me.

"I won't forget you either," he mutters in my ear as if he can hear my thoughts.

I stare back at him, and just as I'm about to say something, the distinct sound of a twig snapping outside steals my words.

The sound of heavy footsteps follows next.

Chapter Fourteen

Nick

uck, they found us.

Damn it. Although I anticipated this happening, I hoped it wouldn't.

I tuck my dick back into my pants, feeling like the asshole again.

Everything about this woman makes me lose focus. I shouldn't have had sex with her again, but I couldn't help myself.

Maybe if I hadn't, I would have heard the men approaching, and I wouldn't feel like this. Like she's gotten deeper under my skin and I don't want her to leave.

I wish we could be anywhere but here in the middle of danger. I can hear the men outside now. It's undoubtedly them.

Tennessee is so terrified, she's shaking.

She puts her clothes back on and shrinks into the wall.

"You stay here and don't make a sound. You hear me?" I keep my voice low.

"Yes. Be careful."

I don't waste time thinking I could be anything other than careful. All I think of is that I have to get her out of this, even if it kills me.

I move on that thought and head up the stairs with my guns ready. I lock the door behind me, although it's not secure. Just like the front door, it's ready to fall off the hinges.

Shadows move around outside the windows while I creep toward the door.

"Go in and look," says a voice I now recognize to be Federico's.

He's here. I should have known he would come and try to end me himself.

It wouldn't be his style to send his people when my hands are still warm with his brother's blood.

As the door opens, I shoot and aim for the heads of the men coming in. I get four of them before the element of surprise fades, and I have to take cover.

The goal is to lure them away from the house. Or rather, the basement.

If I can do that, she'll be safe.

With that reasoning, I crash through the window and open fire at the remaining men. I count ten, but it's dark and I can't see everyone.

I hide behind a tree and shoot from there. They shoot back, and for the first time in my lengthy career as an enforcer, I'm not sure if I'm going to make it.

The men rush at me, luring me into combat, which makes me lose sight of the front door.

Suddenly, we become a clash of punches and kicks as I fight to stay alive to protect her—my girl.

It's a nice thought that I entertain for a moment. It gives me strength. My mother used to tell me the stories about how she met my father. She said it was love at first sight. I never believed it. I still didn't until three nights ago when I met Tennessee Patterson.

I believed it then because I experienced it.

Summoning everything inside me, I take out the first two guys. As they fall, I shoot another two and round back to shoot the first to ensure they never move again.

I retrieve my other gun and fire both.

Moments later, all that remains before me are dead men.

But where is Federico?

"Where the fuck are you, Federico!" I shout. "Come out and face me!"

"Right here. I'm right here," he answers in a sing-song voice, and to my horror, he comes out of the cottage with Tennessee, his gun held to her head.

Tears stream down her cheeks, glistening on her pretty face in the moonlight.

Federico smiles when he sees me. I can't hide the crestfallen look on my face any more than I can push aside the guilt crippling me.

He got her.

"This is nice. A sweet country girl," Federico taunts.

"You fucking let her go."

"Why would I, when this is about killing her?"

She starts crying harder.

He cocks the hammer, and I realize I have less than a second to do something.

Anything.

So, I do the only thing I can, and hope I can be faster than him.

I cock my hammer, too, on both guns, and shoot him in his head and neck.

The impact takes him down instantly, so he doesn't even get to pull the trigger.

Tennessee drops to her knees as he falls, and I rush up to her, holding her.

Her arms circle me, and I feel her heart beating against mine.

She feels like mine again. I allow myself to think it for a few moments, and when they pass, I accept the reality that this is it.

This time when we part, it will be goodbye. When you love someone, you have to know when to let go, and she will never be safe if she's with me.

Chapter Fifteen

Tennessee

It's nearly ten when we pull up on the drive of Georgia's house.

I never thought I would see the place again.

Nick guessed right that the men in the woods would have gotten there in some sort of transport. When we searched around, we found motorcycles in a clearing near the river two miles away from the cottage.

We took one and rode out of the woods like we had the fires of Hell chasing us.

I'm home now. A whole day has passed, and I feel like I've been on some crazy adventure. It also doesn't seem like Georgia is home yet. Her car isn't here, and the lights are all off. The door is also locked, which means someone must have done that because we left it open.

Nick helps me off the motorcycle and steadies me when I stumble.

I grip his hands and gaze up at him, taking note of the sadness in his eyes.

"Thanks. I guess I'm a little wobbly still."

"That's understandable."

"Thank you for saving me. It's not how I imagined seeing you again, but hey…"

He lifts a lock of my hair and looks at the ends brushing over his palm. "How did you imagine it?"

"It's crazy. In my head, I was thinking you'd take me up on the offer to try my cookies because they really are the best. But then I realized I would never see you again that way because you don't look like you've ever eaten sugar in your life."

He grins. "But I had you, sweet Tennessee."

"Me?"

"Yes. You. And this was definitely not how I imagined seeing you again."

"How did you imagine it?" I find myself smiling, as if the last twenty-four hours never happened.

"I'd take you up on that offer to have your cookies. Then I'd take you to Italy and feast on you under the moonlight forever."

A moment of light passes between us, and he dips his head to kiss me.

The kiss is sweet and soothing. It whispers over every part of my body, telling me secrets of desire, but when he pulls away from my lips, I know this is the end.

"It's best I go now." His voice is low and filled with remorse and regret. The kind of remorse and regret you feel when you stop yourself from seizing an opportunity you know could change everything.

I know it all too well because that's how I feel.

"Now? You have to leave right now?" My voice breaks. "Don't you want to come in and rest for the night? It's so late."

"I know, but it's better if I go and you get back to your life."

My gaze drops briefly to the space between us.

"I'm not going to see you again, am I?"

"No."

My heart hurts. It physically aches at the thought of this final moment.

"I..."

"Bellezza, if you hadn't met me, you wouldn't have needed saving today. It's as simple as that. You'll be safe now. I'll make sure of that." He steps away from me, and I feel like something shattered around us, breaking the spell. "Goodbye, Tennessee."

"Goodbye...Nick." As the words fall from my lips, my heart shatters, too.

I swore I would never love again, but I didn't realize I hadn't begun to love yet until I met the man who would risk his life to save mine.

Chapter Sixteen

Nick

One month later...

Leo rests his hands on my desk and grins at me.

"What now?" I snap.

"Working late again?"

"Something like that." I move the papers next to me and stare back at him knowing he's going to take a dig at me again.

When we're not on the streets, we're at D'Agostinos Inc. acting like normal people who have a day job. We do the security checks for Massimo on his new clients.

"So, let me guess. I'll go home, and you'll pretend you're working, but really, you're checking up on her."

Her—Tennessee.

Since we both know how I spend most nights when I'm here late, I won't pretend I don't know what he's talking about.

Every now and again—which is practically every other day—I look in on her to see if she's okay. That's it. That's all I do.

There's no threat from anyone, and she's safe. It's just me finding it hard to let her go.

"There's no harm in it."

"There's no harm in being with her either." Leo nods.

"I don't know how you can say that to me. Look what happened."

"And you fixed it. Now look at the state of you. Have you ever thought that maybe the reason you can't get this woman out of your head is because she's supposed to stay there?"

"No, I haven't." I chuckle. "I need to move on. She's not safe with a guy like me."

"Do you know how many of us could say shit like that? We all could. I would never meet a woman like that and try to move on. Move on to what?"

He couldn't be more right, but I dare not entertain the thought.

"I just have to. She's better off without me. I care enough about her to want her to live a happy, normal life with whomever she meets next."

"Alright, if you really, honestly, truly believe that, and you know you can let her go, then move on. But if you don't believe it, she's not going to leave your head any time soon, so you might as well be with her." He pulls in a breath and leaves me.

I stare at the empty trail he leaves behind and think about what he said.

It's so tempting to jump on the next plane and head to Charlotte. I've held back for the last month, but it's proven harder than I ever anticipated. Since I last saw her, I've found myself falling harder for her.

It's her birthday in two days, and I've thought of all the things I would have done to spoil her if I were with her.

Leo doesn't know what the fuck he's talking about half the time, but for the other half, he does. Tonight, he was more than right, so I can admit that Tennessee Patterson isn't leaving my head any time soon. And that doesn't mean I couldn't let her go because I didn't love her enough.

Do I think she'd be safer without me?

Yes.

Do I think she could live a happy, normal life with some other guy?

Absolutely.

But do I want some other guy making her happy?

No, because I want to.

I'd spend the rest of my life trying to make her happy, and I would keep her safe.

I know that, so why am I allowing fear to rule me?

Chapter Seventeen

Tennessee

"I thought we would go somewhere and celebrate your birthday properly," Georgia bubbles.

I shake my head and continue wiping down the counter of the display unit, showing off the cakes I made today. There are a few slices left, and I'm sure they'll all be gone by closing time.

The shop has been busy today. The only time I wasn't here was when I had lunch with the girls. They're all here for the weekend, so we can hang out then. I'm not in the mood to do anything besides go home and sleep.

I'm thirty-two, and I feel like I'm ninety-two years old. Two weeks ago, we bought a cat, and I spend more time with it than I do outside.

I'm just broken, and I know it's crazy because I didn't know Nick long enough for him to cut me so deeply. But he did.

"Hey, are you still thinking about him?" Georgia gives me a sympathetic smile.

"Yeah. I'll be fine, though. You should go see James." That's her new love interest. He's a surfer, so I think he might be a keeper. Georgia loves men who love the water.

"Don't be ridiculous. I'm not leaving you here on your birthday."

"We've hung out all day. It's a few hours until closing time. I'll help the staff close up."

The door opens, and we both look over to see Kurt walking in holding a large bouquet of red roses.

I stifle a groan and try to tamp down my annoyance. This is the third time this week he's been here. His firm has an office in Charlotte, and since I've moved here, he's been around more.

Earlier today, Mama came by, too. No doubt she saw him and put him up to this.

"What do you want?" Georgia snaps at him.

"It's my wife's birthday. I've come to bring her flowers and take her to dinner."

"Don't that sound fancy?" Sarcasm ripples through her voice. "Kurt, you're the last person my cousin wants to eat with, and she doesn't want your stupid flowers, either. So why don't you take them and shove the bunch of 'em right up your ass."

"So classy, Georgia." He gives her a haughty glare.

"I don't care what you say to me."

"Georgia, please. I got this," I cut in before she can continue. My cousin always has my back. I love her for it, but I know when I need to speak up for myself so I don't appear weak. This is one of those times.

"Alright. I'll be out back, if you need me."

She struts toward the breakroom, throwing daggers at Kurt right up until she walks through the door. Once the door clicks shut, I return my focus to him.

"Shouldn't those flowers be for Mary?" I ask. "Or the stripper you've been dating?"

The bastard looks thrown off kilter. "What stripper, baby?"

"Kurt, please leave and leave me alone." I don't need to put up with him anymore. He disgusts me. "If you're going to deny the stripper that everybody knows about, that's fine, but I don't think you can deny the woman who just had your child." Mary gave birth to his son a few days ago, so he really shouldn't be here.

"I wasn't. I was hoping we could talk."

"There's nothing to talk about. I don't want you."

"Look at you. You're a mess. You need me. You're not going to make it out here without me. You aren't clever enough to run a business."

My cheeks burn with embarrassment, but I stand my ground. "You never knew me."

"Of course, I knew you. That's why I'm telling you you're setting yourself up for a fall. What you need to do is come back home and be my wife. We can sort out this mess."

"You're deluded if you think this can be sorted out. You and Mary just had a child."

"I know, but I still want you back."

"I don't want you." It's amazing how I've never considered taking him back. Maybe because I knew he'd only end up hurting me again. Apart from Mary, the stripper wasn't the only woman I've heard about hanging off his arm. During the months we've been apart, there have been several. "I've moved on. You need to do the same and leave me alone."

He laughs. "Moved on to what? Who the hell do you think is going to want a woman who can't have kids?"

"Me," comes a voice from the doorway. The voice I thought I'd only be hearing in my dreams for the rest of my life.

Nick's here in my world again, saving me in another way.

Dressed in full black, he looks like the Dark Knight. *My* dark knight. And he's here.

His hair has grown slightly longer, and so has his beard, but he's even more handsome than I remember.

"Who the hell are you?" Kurt challenges, looking like a weakling when Nick walks inside the shop.

The only claim to being athletic Kurt had was when he played football in high school. He didn't completely lose his physique, but he looks nothing like Nick, who is slightly older.

"My name is Nick Bellotto, and I'm who Tennessee has moved on to, so I don't really appreciate that shit you've said to her."

"It's the truth."

"Then you really never knew her, *Kurt.* This woman is strong and beautiful. She's intelligent and witty, and most of all, she knows her worth. That's why she's not taking you back. I can only hope I make her and all the children we'll adopt as happy as they deserve to be."

Oh my God, what is he saying? I can't take my eyes off him. He's looking at me, too, and I can see he's serious. Everything that came out of his mouth was true.

"I didn't know Tennessee had anybody like that in her life."

Nick walks up to Kurt and squares off with him. "She does, and we're about to head to Italy for her birthday. So, *Kurt*, you need to leave her alone and never come back. Believe me, you don't want a problem with me. Capisce?"

The intimidation is clear. I know Kurt well enough to notice when he feels threatened. He's exactly that now, and since he knows what battles to fight, he also knows when to fall back.

"Capisce," Kurt replies.

He cuts me a hard look, then he leaves, and I feel free. Finally...

I look back at Nick, and I can't resist skipping into his arms. He picks me up, spins me around, and kisses me, then sets me back down.

"You are one hell of a surprise," I beam.

"Happy birthday, Bellezza. Ready to go?"

I laugh, and it's great to feel like myself again. "Go where?"

"You heard me. Our flight to Florence leaves in an hour."

I stare back at him in disbelief. "You're serious? You're actually serious?"

He cups my face. "I am, about everything."

"Everything? Nick, you were talking about kids." I laugh again, but damn does my heart ever hope with longing for the fantasy he just spoke of.

"I meant everything. I went back to L.A., and I couldn't get you out of my head, then I realized I didn't want to. I decided to come here to be with you, but I want more than just to make you mine. I want everything. We didn't have the best beginning, and I never wanted to put you in danger, but if you'll have me, I promise to treat you like my queen, love you forever, and keep you safe."

Tears tip over my lids, and joy bubbles within me, making me feel whole.

"I want nothing more than to be with you, but only if you let me love you back."

He gives me that sexy smile that dreams are made of and plants a kiss on my forehead.

"That sounds like a good deal to me."

"Me too."

Epilogue

Tennessee

One year later

Nick traces a line of kisses up my leg.

Under the moonlit Tuscan sky, he carries that Dark Knight vibe again.

"How do you taste sweeter than those cookies?" he teases, licking the inside of my thigh.

"Only to you."

"It's true, Bellezza, and I'm going to taste you everywhere."

"I'll hold you to that."

We got married this morning in the old vineyard. Today

has been the best birthday I've ever had. All our friends and family were here to celebrate with us.

Even Mama looked like she'd finally decided to stop making my life hell. It hardly matters because I have the man of my dreams, and that's all I care about.

Now Nick has me naked and sprawled out on a blanket. Every time he takes me to Italy, we do this. But this time, we'll be making love under the stars as husband and wife.

He lowers his head to claim my lips, and I get lost in his kiss the way I did when we said, 'I do.'

As we took our vows this morning, it felt like I was renewing my soul.

I knew I'd have forever with this man, and he would have me, too.

We'd belong to each other and create our own happily ever after.

* * *

THANKS SO MUCH FOR READING. I HOPE YOU ENJOYED THIS STORY.

To check out my dark mafia world, start with Ruthless Prince, the first book in the Dark Syndicate series.

Acknowledgments

For my readers.
Always for you.
Thank you for reading my stories.
I hope you continue to enjoy my wild adventures xx

About the Author

Faith Summers is the Dark Contemporary Romance pen name of USA Today Bestselling Author, Khardine Gray. Warning !! Expect wild romance stories of the scorching hot variety and deliciously dark romance with the kind of alpha male bad boys best reserved for your fantasies. Dive in and enjoy her naughty page-turners.

9 781915 383662